Nina
Fairy Ballerina

Glitter Club

Anna Wilson

Illustrated by Nicola Slater

MACMILLAN CHILDREN'S BOOKS

First published 2007 by Macmillan Children's Books
a division of Macmillan Publishers Limited
20 New Wharf Road, London N1 9RR
Basingstoke and Oxford
www.panmacmillan.com

Associated companies throughout the world

ISBN: 978-0-230-01537-1

1 3 5 7 9 8 6 4 2

A CIP catalogue record for this book is available from
the British Library.

Typeset by Nigel Hazle
Printed and bound in Great Britain by Mackays of Chatham plc, Kent

For Nellie Nougat (and Fred,
even though you'll never read this!)
— oh, and those parents of yours too, I suppose
✗✗✗

Chapter One

Bella, Nina and their friends were sitting cross-legged on the floor of the Grand Hall in the Royal Academy of Fairy Ballet. They were focused on their headmistress, Madame Dupré.

"I'm sure it has not escaped your notice that the half-term holidays are coming up," she was saying. "And now that you are in your Second Year, I think it would be fun to set you a few challenges . . ."

Nyssa Bean groaned quietly and whispered, "Holidays are supposed to be for relaxing!"

Nina nudged her and said, "Shh!"

The headmistress continued. "I thought it would be a lovely idea for you to join the Glitter Club."

The fairies murmured, "What's that?"

Madame Dupré smiled. "Ah, you have a great treat in store, my dears! The Glitter Club is for all young fairies who like to have adventures and fun. You will learn a lot about friendship and teamwork too."

"Dull or what?" muttered Nyssa quietly.

Madame held up a slim gold chain. "When you join the club, each of you will be presented with a necklace like this," she explained.

The fairies perked up and even Nyssa started to pay attention.

"Every time you complete a challenge you will earn a beautiful gem to wear on your chain. If, for example, you wish to work towards the Dancer Gem, then you need to look that up in the Glitter Club Gem Book —" Madame put down the necklace and showed her pupils a booklet with pictures of the gems — "and read about what you need to do to achieve this gem. The Dancer Gem is a sapphire," she said, pointing to an image of a dazzling blue jewel. "I have here some copies of the Glitter Club Gem Book for you all. You may take them away with you later and decide which gem you would like to try and earn over the half-term holiday."

Nina was very taken with the picture of the sapphire. She knew at once that she had to win it.

Madame started handing round the

books and explained what the fairies had to do to join the Glitter Club.

"Before you can start earning the gems, there will be a Welcoming Ceremony here at the Academy. During the ceremony you will make some promises and then you will receive your golden chain. Your families will, of course, be very welcome to attend the ceremony," said the headmistress.

Later that day, back in her room on Charlock corridor, Nina was flicking eagerly through her Glitter Club Gem Book with Nyssa and discussing what she had to do to get the Dancer Gem.

Nyssa had changed her mind about the club being dull and was saying how she wanted to do the Cook's Gem, which was a ruby.

"It's a shame Peri's not here. She'd love all this," said Nina, suddenly feeling sad that her old friend wasn't at the Academy any more. "She could do the Actor's Gem

standing on her head! I was hoping to see her this half-term, but the Stage School doesn't have the same holiday dates as us," she added quietly.

At that moment, Bella burst into the room, waving some envelopes in the air.

"I've already made a start on my gem!" she announced, beaming. Then, "Oh dear," she said, stopping in her tracks at the sight of her friend moping. "What's up?"

"Just thinking about Peri," said Nina.

"Oh, yeah . . ." said Bella, but she couldn't stay serious for long – she was too eager to talk about the gem she wanted. "This will cheer you up!" she said, chucking a pink envelope at each of her friends. "I want to go for the Hostess Gem. It's an emerald."

Nyssa excitedly tore open her envelope. Inside was a pink invitation decorated with stars:

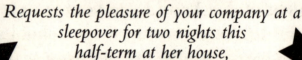

Bella Glove

Requests the pleasure of your company at a sleepover for two nights this half-term at her house,

Begonia Manor

Please bring a sleeping bag, PJs and your

Glitter Club Gem Books

"Yippeee!" shouted Nyssa. "I haven't ever had a sleepover for one night, let alone *two*!"

"It's going to be fab," said Bella. "I've invited Coriander and Poppy too."

Nina was reading her invitation with a worried look on her face.

"What's the matter, Nina?" asked Bella impatiently. "Don't you want to come?"

"Of course I want to!" her friend replied. "It's just . . . well, how are Nyssa and I going to get *our* gems if we're staying at your house?" Nina asked.

Bella laughed. "Oh, I've already thought of that. You can do your tasks as part of the sleepover! Nina, you could go for your Dancer Gem by dancing for us – it says in the book that a hostess needs to provide entertainment. And as your hostess I am officially booking you as our entertainment," she said with a bow. "Which gem do you want to do, Nyssa?"

"The Cook's Gem," Nyssa replied.

"Great! You can cook yummy food for a

feast – we'll have it at midnight on the last night!" Bella said decisively.

Nina smiled. "Looks like you've got everything covered," she said. "We can't really say no, can we?"

Chapter Two

The morning before the half-term holidays, the Second-Year fairy ballerinas assembled in the Grand Hall with their families and friends. Rows and rows of golden chairs had been set out for the audience. When everyone was ready, Madame Dupré instructed the Second Years to come up to the stage and form a fairy ring by holding hands. Then she led them in the Glitter Club rhyme that they had been practising since Madame had told them about the club:

Glitter Girls promise to work as a team
And never use magic to cheat.
To each own a Glitter Gem – this is our
dream
And we'll strive to achieve this great feat.

As the last word rang out across the Grand
Hall, a fine mist of silvery white fairy dust
appeared in the air, settling on the fairy
ballerinas' heads and shoulders. Then there
was a burst of light, like the sun appearing
from behind a dark cloud after a rainstorm.
The fairies jumped and blinked furiously.
But the light soon faded, and then the
ballerinas gasped as did the whole audience,
for the walls and ceiling of the Grand Hall
were now coated in glittering jewels of
different colours. Also, hovering above the
circle of fairy ballerinas was a new fairy.
She was dressed in a shimmering costume,
encrusted with jewels similar to the ones
now lining the hall. On her head she wore a
tiara also made of gemstones.

Madame Dupré smiled at the rows of
surprised faces and stepped outside the
ring. She gestured to the new arrival and
announced, "Please give a warm welcome
to Precious Gem from the Glitter Club."

Precious curtseyed to the Second
Years and then to the audience while still
hovering in the air, and then
she spoke.

"Good
morning,
everyone. I
am delighted
to be here to
welcome you to the
club. Please come
into the middle of
the circle one at
a time to
make your
promise."

Bella was
first. She went

shyly into the centre of the fairy ring and Precious spun her gently round, telling her to look carefully at every one of the jewels on the walls. And as Bella turned, she said these words:

Twist me and turn me and show me each gem –
I promise to work hard to earn one of them!

As soon as the rhyme was completed, there was a flash of gold light at Bella's throat and

a gold chain appeared round her neck. She
stared at it – it was so delicate, such fine
fairy gold. She thanked Precious and took
her place back in the fairy ring, so that
Nina could go and make her promise.

At last, all the Second Years had their
gold necklaces. They curtseyed to Precious,
and she smiled and said, "Welcome to the
Glitter Club, fairies! Look after your chains
and read your Gem Books carefully so that
you know how to earn the gem of your
choice. Ask a grown-up to check that you
have done everything properly. Then turn to
the Gem Spell at the back of the book and
say this with a grown-up, and the beautiful
jewel will appear by magic on your gold
chain. I hope you'll have fun completing
your challenges. But remember: neither
you nor any member of your family may
use magic to help you. You *must* keep your
Glitter Club promise, because if you don't,
you may lose your golden chains and your
gems forever."

Nina felt at her neck for the shiny
necklace and repeated the promise again
silently to herself. She couldn't wait to get
started on earning that sapphire!

Chapter Three

After the Welcoming Ceremony, Nina met her sister, Poppy, to take her to Bella's house, and Bella rushed to get Princess Coriander. The friends gathered at the front gates of the Academy, where Nyssa was already waiting for them on a private dragonfly sent by Bella's mum, Foxy, to take them to Begonia Manor.

The journey took most of the day. The dragonfly wove its way through fields and woods and along the bank of a silvery stream as the fairies ate their packed lunches, chatted and snoozed. Eventually, as

the sun was setting, Begonia Manor came
into view – a huge mansion built in an old
sycamore stump, with glistening fairy lights
lighting up the dusk.

"Who's that?" asked Coriander as they alighted.

A fairy was standing on the steps of the big house, waiting for the ballerinas to arrive. She looked older than Nina and her friends.

"You didn't tell us you had a sister!" said Nina, surprised. She turned to Bella and saw that her friend did not look at all pleased to see this other fairy.

"I *haven't*," said Bella through gritted teeth. "That's my cousin – Catkin Moss."

Bella couldn't say any more, as Catkin was already sauntering to meet her and her friends. The fairy sashayed gracefully down the steps in her high-heeled boots and flicked her long dark silky hair over her shoulders, fluttering her silvery wings a little. Nina noticed Catkin had the same almond-shaped eyes as Bella.

"Bellaaaa," said the glamorous fairy, kissing the air either side of Bella's head and saying, "Mwah, mwah," as she did so.

"Yeah, hi," Bella replied awkwardly. "What are you doing here?" she added sullenly as the friends trooped into the house.

"Charming! What I'm 'doing here', as you so graciously put it, is looking after *you*. Auntie Foxy had to rush off to a performance at the last minute and she asked me to babysit you lot, because Mum can't do it. Mum's a fashion designer, you know," she said to Bella's awestruck friends. "She's always *terribly* busy."

"Aren't you supposed to be at college?" Bella asked.

"We've got study leave," Catkin replied airily. "I go to the Fairy Fashion School," she said to the others, swishing her dark mane of hair with a toss of her head. "Anyway, Mum says you're working towards your Hostess Gem this half-term . . ." she continued, enjoying the look of horror that passed over Bella's face as she said this.

"What do *you* know about the Hostess

Gem?" Bella exclaimed. "You're not a member of the Glitter Club too, are you?"

"You must be joking!" Catkin retorted. "I wouldn't be seen dead wearing one of those ugly little chains," she continued, flicking Bella's gold Glitter Club necklace disdainfully. "And as for those vulgar gems . . . no way! Mum was always trying to get me to join when I was *your* age," she

continued, smirking at the other fairies, "but I had better things to do."

Bella was trying hard to ignore her cousin's manner. But Catkin still went on and on.

"Mum's *great* friends with the president. What's her name – Precious Stone or something."

"Precious *Gem* actually," said Bella huffily. Her cousin was such a show-off!

"Yeah, whatever," said Catkin, waving her hand dismissively. "It's all boring anyway. I'm going to my room now. Mum's away till tomorrow, so it'll be me tucking you up tonight," she went on with a sugary smile. "Mum said she'd be back tomorrow afternoon to check you've done everything you need to get your tedious little gems." She gave a sneer, and fluttered off to her room.

Poppy waited until Catkin was out of earshot and then, striking a pose and flicking her hair about, she mimicked the

older fairy: "Oh, daaaarling, aren't I just the
perfect example of a stuck-up nightmare on
wings—"

"Poppy!" Nina scolded her sister, but
couldn't help smiling.

Bella and Nyssa were bent double
with laughter. "Poppy, that's
a brilliant impression!"
Bella squeaked.
Coriander
joined in, not
to be outdone:
"I'm at Fashion
School, you know,"
she sneered, pouting
and preening exactly like
Catkin. "Well, *someone*
has to teach me
about style!"
The friends fell into
Bella's bedroom
in a giggling
heap.

Chapter Four

Bella's room was beautiful. Three of the walls were painted lilac and the fourth wall had a mural of a forest scene on it. It was so lifelike that Nina felt she could have walked right into it and sat under a tree. Against one of the lilac walls was the bed, which was a large four-poster with a silver muslin curtain draped over it. The curtain had tiny purple flowers embroidered on it and there was a pretty, thick, soft duvet on the bed and loads of plump cushions.

"Wow, Bella! Your room is so cool!"

Nyssa gushed, staring open-mouthed at everything.

"Where are our beds?" asked Poppy, dumping down her rucksack. "I'm not sleeping on the floor!"

"Me neither!" said Coriander.

Bella rolled her eyes. "Give us a chance! I'll get you some camp beds."

"Camp beds – fab!" said Poppy, jumping up and down. "Not that I'm planning on doing much sleeping . . ." she added, a twinkle in her eye.

"We should all get a good night's sleep tonight if we're going to work for our gems tomorrow," said Nina sensibly.

"Boring!" Coriander shouted, taking a flying leap at Bella's bed. "Whoever heard of getting a good night's sleep on a sleepover?" she cried, hurling a cushion at Nina.

"Hey! Cori – careful," said Bella, laughing nervously. "I don't want Catkin coming in and telling us to keep quiet."

"Great!" Poppy exclaimed sulkily. "So

now Miss Fancy Pants is looking after us, we can't have any fun. Some sleepover this is going to be."

"You could always go home, Poppy," Nina snapped.

"Erm, where are those camp beds, Bella?" asked Nyssa, stepping in to break up the tension. "Let's get unpacked and sort out who's sleeping where, shall we?"

Bella smiled at her friend gratefully and asked everyone to help her. The beds were folded away into a large silver-birch wardrobe in the corner of the room. Soon everyone was busy setting them up and rolling out their sleeping bags. By now it was dark outside, so the fairies decided to change into their pyjamas.

But Poppy wasn't keen to go to bed yet. "I'm starving!" she announced. "I ate all my sandwiches ages ago. I don't suppose your crabby cousin has got any supper for us, has she?"

Bella sighed. "Probably not. But it

doesn't matter – I'm your hostess, so I'm in charge of the food tonight! Let's hit the kitchen."

The friends eagerly fluttered down the stairs with Bella in the lead. She showed them a huge fly-in larder at the back of the kitchen and said they could help themselves to whatever they wanted. Then she grabbed a tray so that they could take their snacks back to her room.

Poppy was in heaven, fluttering around the shelves, pulling down packets of biscuits, mini fairy cakes, colourful sweets and sesame buns. Nina helped Nyssa make some peppermint tea, and Coriander mixed some dandelion cordial. They stacked the tray high with goodies and carefully carried it back to Bella's bedroom to enjoy their feast.

"This is fab!" Poppy sighed contentedly as she crammed her mouth full of goodies. "Mum would never let us eat this at home!"

Bella grinned. "Mum only lets me have

stuff like this for treats, but she's not here, is she? And what she doesn't know can't hurt her!"

The friends laughed and gossiped as they worked their way through all the food. They were polishing off the last few crumbs, when Catkin poked her head round the door.

"Lights out!" she said bossily.

"We're on holiday – leave us alone," said Bella crossly as she hurled an empty cake wrapper at her cousin.

Catkin narrowed her eyes. "With pleasure. You can't possibly imagine I have the slightest interest in your little party anyway," she said over her shoulder as she flew off.

Bella breathed a sigh of relief. "So, I was thinking: I'm going to make some decorations for this room tomorrow, but I can't decide on a theme. What dance are you doing for your gem, Nina?"

"I don't know yet," Nina confessed. "I've brought some ballet stories with me – shall we have a look through them now?"

"Count me out; I'm getting sleepy," said Coriander, yawning. "I might just snuggle up and listen to you read," she added, grinning lazily.

"Yeah, read us a story, Nina!" Bella cried.

The fairies cleaned their teeth and

clambered into their sleeping bags. Nina
flicked through her ballet book to find
a good story to read. They all looked so
wonderful she found it hard to choose, but
at last she decided on "The Firebird". She
cleared her throat to start reading, but her
friends were all fast asleep!

Chapter Five

The fairies woke early, eager to start working for their gems. After breakfast, Bella said Nina could practise her dance in her bedroom.

"We can put the camp beds away for now," she said, and began folding them as the others rolled up their sleeping bags.

Bella asked Coriander if she wanted to help her find fabrics, paper and ribbons to make the decorations with.

But Coriander wanted to help Nina. "What does it say in the Glitter Club Gem

Book about the Dancer Gem?" she asked
her.

Nina read:

1. *Choose a ballet that you are not familiar
    with*
2. *Make up your own dance based on the story
    of that ballet*
3. *Perform to a piece of music on Daisy Disc*

"Have you chosen a ballet yet?" Bella
asked. "I want to know what to do for the
decorations."

"I chose the story last night," Nina
replied. "It's called 'The Firebird' – it's
lovely."

"Oh yes, that's a great story," Bella
agreed. "I've got a Daisy Disc of the music,
as it happens. I'll get it for you." She flew
over to her bedside table, and started
rummaging through a pile of discs.

"I don't know the story," said Coriander.

"Don't worry, it's probably boring,"

muttered Poppy, who preferred adventure stories to fairy tales.

Nina glared at her sister and then told Coriander, "It's not boring at all. It's very romantic. A Russian prince called Ivan is out hunting one day when he sees the most beautiful bird with bright red feathers," she began. "He catches it to take it back to his palace—"

"That's so cruel!" cried Coriander. "He can't have been a real prince. Real princes are much kinder than that."

"It's only a story, silly!" said Nina kindly. "Anyway, it turns out the Firebird is actually a magic bird. She begs the prince to free her and, when he agrees, she gives him one of her feathers and tells him that if ever he's in trouble, he can wave the feather and she'll come and help him."

"How can a bird help a prince?" Poppy asked grumpily. "All the ballet stories you tell me are rubbish, Nina! It's all talking dolls and dying swans and people sleeping for hundreds of years."

Nina scowled. "Anyway," she continued, "it turns out the prince *does* need the bird's help, because he has to rescue a beautiful princess from a wizard and some monsters—"

"Hey, a beautiful princess – this story's getting better!" Coriander interrupted, fluttering her eyelashes.

Nina laughed and continued. "The prince calls to the Firebird and she comes and casts a spell on the wizard and the monsters and sends them to sleep. While they are asleep, the bird tells the prince to hunt for an egg that contains the wizard's soul. He finds it and breaks it. The wizard and the monsters die, and the prince and princess marry—"

"And live happily ever after!" Poppy finished sarcastically.

Bella saw the irritated look on Nina's face and said quickly, "Sounds fab! I reckon I could make some Firebird decorations to hang on the walls in here."

"Lovely!" said Nina, ignoring her little sister.

"I hope I don't have to make bird food," said Nyssa anxiously.

"No way!" Poppy exclaimed. "You won't catch me eating birdseed—"

"Poppy!" Nina cried.

"It's all right, Poppy," said Bella. "We'll pretend our Firebird eats chocolate! Off you go with Nyssa to the kitchen."

Poppy followed Nyssa out of the room, but stopped to pull a face at her sister as she went.

"Honestly, Poppy Dewdrop," said Nina, sounding exactly like her mum, "you are a handful."

Chapter Six

Once Nyssa and Poppy had gone, Bella announced that she was going up to the attic to hunt through her mum's old dance costumes for fabric she could use for the decorations.

"Peace at last!" said Nina. "I hope Poppy's not going to ruin everything . . . Coriander, can you be in charge of the music?" she asked, handing Coriander the disc Bella had found.

Nina decided she would base her dance on the scene where the Firebird is first spotted by the prince, flying through the forest.

"Can you find the right track for me? Now . . . Look at that forest scene on Bella's mural," Nina told Coriander. "Let's listen to the music and try to imagine a bird swooping down through the branches of the trees."

Coriander found the right track on the disc and the two friends sat on the floor, staring at the painting on the wall. They let themselves be carried away by the dreamy music, imagining the brilliant red bird weaving in and out of the forest.

The track finished and Nina turned to Coriander, smiling. "So, what do you reckon?" she asked. "How can I make myself move like a bird?"

"Well, obviously you can't really fly," said Coriander thoughtfully. She had been at the Academy long enough to know that a fairy ballerina must never use her wings to cheat.

"Of course," Nina agreed. "I'll have to

practise some jumps, but first I need to think of how I can link one jump to the next. What about if I start with a 'pas couru'?" she said.

"What's that?" asked Coriander.

"It's a run that you can use as a joining step or as a preparation for a jump. Miss Bliss taught us a few ways to link movements last term when she told us about the 'pas de deux' in *The Nutcracker*. We've done more work on it since. Let's see . . ."

She stood in first position and closed her eyes, trying hard to remember what her teacher had told her.

"I need to make my arms look like wings, since I can't use my own!" As she said this, Nina went into a "pas dégagé", sliding her left foot out in front of her, and pointing it in an open position. Her knee was slightly bent in a "demi-plié" and her right foot was turned out, supporting her body. Then she gracefully inclined her

head to look
down, keeping
her neck long.
She held her
arms softly in front
of her in an oval
shape, as if she was
resting her hands on
a beautiful full skirt.
Then she rose up from
this position on to "demi-
pointe" and smoothly slid
into a little run. As she
ran, she made tiny steps
and moved her arms
away from her body
as if she was pushing
the invisible skirt away from her. Coriander
thought she looked like a bird, gliding
through a fine mist on a frosty autumn
morning.

"That's fantastic, Nina!" she cried,
clapping her hands.

Then, without warning, Nina picked up speed and soared up with her arms held out high on either side, and her legs stretched as if she was doing the splits in the air! She seemed to hover at the highest point of the jump and then gently floated down into fifth position, ending in a demi-plié that was so soft, Coriander thought Nina might vanish like a melting snowflake.

"Wow," said the princess simply. "I've never seen anyone at the Academy jump like that."

Nina blushed. "Thanks," she said. "It's a new jump I've been practising. It's called a 'sissonne fondue' – it means you must look as though you are melting away at the end."

"That's *exactly* what it looked like!" cried Coriander excitedly. "I think you should try it with the music."

"OK," said Nina. She watched Coriander fiddle with the Daisy Discplayer. The princess found the right track again and pressed "Play" – and some blue sparks crackled around her finger, making her jump back.

"Ow!" she cried, shaking her hand. "How did that happen? I got some kind of electric shock from the 'Play' button. I hope I haven't broken anything, Nina," she added anxiously, turning to look at her friend.

The little princess got a proper shock when she saw her friend – Nina was staring terrified at a huge red bird who was towering over her menacingly.

"HELP!" the friends screamed.

Chapter Seven

While Nina was dancing, Nyssa and Poppy were in the kitchen, hovering along the shelves in the larder, collecting the ingredients they needed.

"Hey, we've got to have chocolate-button seed cakes!" Poppy cried, drooling as she took in the rows and rows of baking ingredients. "And marshmallow muffins!"

Nyssa laughed. "I think I can manage that!"

"Oh, and can we have hot chocolate too?" Poppy pleaded.

"Of course," said Nyssa. "It says in the

Glitter Club Gem Book that I have to make a hot drink," she added. "Let's just check the book to see what else I have to do." She read out loud:

1. *Make two different kinds of cake*
2. *Make a hot drink*
3. *Serve your friends*
4. *Make sure you are clean and hygienic*
5. *Clear up afterwards*

"Easy!" said Poppy. "Let's start with the chocolate cakes. I'll get the chocolate buttons – you get the seeds."

Nyssa laughed. "I wonder why you want to do it that way round?" she teased. "Remember we've got to be hygienic, so no snacking while you cook – I don't want your dirty fingers in my baking, thanks."

"Don't worry, I'll wash my hands as I go along!" Poppy quipped, reaching for a packet of chocolate buttons and greedily tearing it open. She winked at Nyssa as she stuffed a handful of the buttons into her mouth. As she did this, her fingers crackled with blue sparks and she dropped the packet in surprise.

Nyssa was annoyed. "Now look what you've done, Poppy! We haven't even started cooking yet and you've already made a mess. You'll have to sweep them up and throw them away. We can hardly use them if we are going to be clean and hygienic."

"All right!" cried Poppy. "Don't get your wings in a twist. You sound just like my mum!"

Poppy did as she was told and cleared up the mess while Nyssa got on with the cake-mix. Then Poppy went to get another packet of buttons from the cupboard and poured them into the mixture while Nyssa got started on the muffins. To Poppy's horror, the same blue sparks went off as she poured in the chocolate buttons, but she managed to keep her hands steady this time and not spill anything.

This chocolate seems to have a life of its own, Poppy thought.

The fairies put the cakes and muffins in the oven and cleared up the kitchen, singing and giggling as they worked. Poppy had never enjoyed tidying up so much before. Nyssa was astonished at how helpful Poppy was being – she even offered to sweep the floor while Nyssa got the cakes out of the oven!

When Nyssa opened the oven door, the fairies expected the room to be filled with deliciously tempting smells. But the aroma that wafted through the kitchen was disgusting.

"Poppy, come here," said Nyssa, cutting

open a chocolate-button seed cake and eyeing it suspiciously.

"What's the matter?" Poppy stopped what she was doing and fluttered over to Nyssa.

"What did you put in these?" Nyssa asked, sounding angry.

"I did what the recipe said: I put in a packet of buttons," said Poppy defensively.

"Have you been casting one of your silly little spells behind my wings?" Nyssa shouted. "I suppose you wanted to get your own back on me for asking you to clear up that mess—"

"Hold on a sec, I don't know what you're on about," Poppy protested angrily.

"Oh yeah?" retorted Nyssa, her hands on her hips. "So how do you explain this?" she asked, shoving the steaming hot tray of cakes in front of Poppy.

Poppy stared at them. "Urgh!" she cried.

"You were meant to put *chocolate* buttons in the mixture," Nyssa was

shouting. "Not *real* buttons! I'll never get my gem now – these cakes are full of melting plastic!"

Chapter Eight

Bella was singing happily to herself. She had been working hard on her decorations all afternoon. She had found all sorts of lovely fabrics, sequins and feathers in the attic and had taken them into her mum's bedroom to sort out.

"I'm going to make lots of little birds with this," she said to herself, picking up an old red feather boa. "And then I can make them into mobiles and hang them from my bedroom ceiling with these scarves. Now, what shall I do on the walls? I know, I could pin this lovely silver fabric up either

side of my mural to make it look like the
stage of a theatre. Then Nina can come
out from behind one of them and dance in
front of the mural . . ."

She looked up the Hostess Gem in her
Glitter Club Gem Book.

1. *Make an invitation for a party or sleepover*
2. *Organize entertainment*
3. *Decorate the room for the party*
4. *Make sure all your friends feel at home*
5. *Provide refreshments*

"I've done the first bit, the decorations are nearly there and I've left the entertainment and refreshments in capable hands," she said to herself. "All I've got to do now is make sure my guests are happy. That shouldn't be a problem—"

But her thoughts were interrupted by angry shouting.

"I knew you'd only go and muck it all up!" someone was raging.

"It's your fault," said another voice. "You're so bossy!"

Oh no, thought Bella. That sounds like Nyssa and Poppy having an argument. I'd better go and see what's going on . . .

She went out on to the landing to find her friends yelling at one another.

Nyssa flew to Bella to explain what had happened.

"Poppy was trying to poison us all with one of her stupid spells," Nyssa started.

"No I was not! I didn't put those buttons in—"

Poppy was stopped in mid-rant by screaming voices that seemed to come from Bella's bedroom further down the landing.

"Help! Help!"

"Oh no, what now?" Bella asked in exasperation. "Is that Nina? Come on, guys. Follow me."

The fairies entered the room to see a large red bird chasing Nina and Coriander.

"Quick, Bella — do something!" Nina shouted, seeing her friend in the doorway.

Bella was rooted to the spot. She didn't know any magic strong enough to get rid of something so scary. Instead she shouted, "Fly for your lives," turned and bumped straight into Catkin.

With a flick of her wand, Catkin

ordered the bird to
disappear. Poppy
thought she saw a few
blue sparks float up to
the ceiling as the bird vanished, but she was
so confused that she couldn't be sure.

"I shall have to tell Mum about this,"
Catkin said sternly when everyone had
calmed down. "She'll be back soon. You

were supposed to be getting on with your
Glitter Club stuff, not larking about casting
spells and shouting. You won't get your
gems if you misbehave."

Bella exploded angrily at her cousin.
"We weren't doing magic and we're
not going to get them now anyway!
Everything's ruined!" She glared at Catkin
– I bet this is all your fault. Just because I
told you to go away last night—"

"I don't know what you're talking
about," Catkin said defensively. "Still,
we can't have you going back to school
without your precious little gems, can we?"
With a glint in her eye, she quickly waved
her wand and cried:

> *Fairy Magic do your stuff!*
> *Bring yummy food that's good enough*
> *To make sure Nyssa gets her gem.*
> *Help Nina dance her best, and then*
> *Make decorations from this mess*
> *To please their wonderful hostess.*

A stream of blue sparkles flowed out of Catkin's wand into Bella's room.

Nina cried, "NO!" clutching at the gold chain round her neck, but it was too late. In an instant the room was transformed with dazzling decorations and a silver table had appeared in the middle of the room, groaning with delicious party food.

But the fairies hardly noticed any of this, because their Glitter Club chains had vanished.

Chapter Nine

"What have you done, Catkin?" Nina turned on the snooty fairy angrily.

"What's the problem?" Catkin retorted. "You were moaning that everything had gone wrong – well, everything's OK now, isn't it?" she said, pointing at the food and the decorations.

"You know very well everything's not OK!" cried Bella. "You used MAGIC, Catkin, and now our chains have disappeared. You must have known that would happen: you said you knew all about the club!"

55

"Oh diddums, little Bella hasn't got her tacky necklace any more," said Catkin nastily. "Well, I'm glad. You always get everything you want, so it'll teach you a lesson if things don't go your way for once. I didn't want to have to look after you and your pathetic friends anyway."

The row quickly stopped when an older version of Catkin fluttered up the stairs. Nina took in the long dark hair and slender willowy figure and stylish clothes, and guessed it was Catkin's mum, Jasmine.

"Catkin Moss! You were supposed to be looking after Bella and her friends!" said Jasmine accusingly. "What in all fairyland have you been up to?"

Bella whizzed over to her aunt and threw herself gratefully into her slender arms. "Oh, Auntie, it's a disaster!" she cried, and hurriedly filled her aunt in on what had happened.

Jasmine glared at her daughter. "I trusted you to look after Bella and her friends," she said. "You knew they had come for a special sleepover to earn their Glitter Club Gems. You were supposed to make sure they were well prepared, then I was going to say the Gem Spell once I'd checked everything." She turned to Nina and said kindly, "I was so looking forward to seeing you dance, dear." Then she looked at her daughter and said sternly, "I think you had better leave us, Catkin. You've set enough blue sparks flying for one day."

Catkin stuck her nose in the air and took off at top speed, not stopping to explain her actions.

Jasmine sighed heavily. "I can't apologize enough, fairies," she said. "I should have known that Catkin would be cross with me for asking her to look after you. I'm sorry that I left her in charge, but I had to do a fashion show at the last minute."

"It's not your fault, Auntie," said Bella. She faced her friends. "Maybe you should all go home. I'll go and call for a dragonfly."

"No, no!" cried Jasmine. "There's no need to break up the party. I'm sure I can get your chains back for you."

"How in all fairyland are you going to do that?" wailed Bella.

"Well, you didn't *ask* Catkin to use magic to help you, did you?" asked Jasmine.

The fairy ballerinas shook their heads mournfully.

"In that case, I'm sure Precious Gem will give you the benefit of the doubt," said Jasmine.

Bella looked puzzled.

"Precious is a dear friend of mine," Jasmine explained. "We have known each other for years, and she has always said that if ever I needed her in an emergency, all I have to do is call her."

"But it will take her ages to get here, and by then it'll be almost time for us to go home," Bella whined.

"Not necessarily," said Jasmine craftily. She reached into the collar of her shirt and

pulled out a glistening green piece of jade
suspended from a gold chain, which was
similar to the ones the friends had just lost.

"This is *my* gem," Jasmine told them.
"And it has magic powers. Precious gave it
to me. All I have to do is hold it and call out
to her and she'll come."

Just like
the Firebird
and her
magic feather!
thought Nina.

Bella looked
scared. "Will she
tell us off for not stopping
Catkin?" she asked.

Jasmine breathed in sharply and raised
her eyebrows. "The truth is, I can't be
certain what she'll say, but she really is the
only one who can sort this out."

Nina shrugged. "It's got to be worth a
try," she said.

Jasmine asked Nina, Nyssa and Bella to

hold hands to form a fairy ring. Then she raised her wand and called out:

Precious Gem, please come and help
dear Bella and her friends.
They've worked as hard as hard can be
to earn their Glitter Gems.
But thanks to naughty magic spells
each one has lost her chain.
The magic was not theirs at all –
they're innocent, that's plain.

The room filled with the same bright light that had appeared in the Grand Hall at the Welcoming Ceremony. When the light faded, Precious Gem was standing in front of the fairies, dressed as before in her jewel-encrusted outfit, but looking much sterner than she had the first time the friends had seen her.

Chapter Ten

Jasmine quickly filled Precious in on the events that had led to the fairies losing their Glitter Club necklaces.

Precious folded her arms and looked hard at the friends. She could see how upset they were, so she sighed and said, "Strictly speaking I should not give you another chance. But, as my dear friend Jasmine has spoken on your behalf, I am willing to give you the benefit of the doubt." She waved her wand as she said this and, with a flash of golden light, Nina, Nyssa and Bella had their chains restored to them. In the same

instant, Bella's room was returned to normal
– the decorations, the chairs and the table
covered with party food disappeared.

"Oh, thank you! Thank you!" they
chorused, and rushed to hug Jasmine, and
Precious, who was rather taken aback.

"All right, fairies," she said, readjusting
her crown and smoothing down her dress.
"If it's all right with you, Jasmine, I would
love to stay so we can catch up on all our
news."

Jasmine was thrilled and took her friend
off to find Catkin while the fairies rushed
to start their work all over again. There was
not much of the day left! However, the
prospect of getting their chains back made
the fairies work harder than before, and it
wasn't long before Bella had made all the
decorations, Poppy and Nyssa had finished
their cooking, and Nina was ready to
dance.

Bella went to fetch Jasmine and Precious,
who appeared dragging a sullen-looking

Catkin with them. Jasmine whispered to
her daughter to "behave herself", and then
looked around approvingly at the wonderful
mobiles and streamers that Bella had put up
on the ceiling and walls.

"This looks glorious, Bella!" she said,
beaming. "Oh, Nina dear – I thought you
might like this for your dance. Catkin tells
me you're going to be a red bird?" She
handed Nina a splendid red dress with
ruffles and frills. "I designed it myself," she
added. Nina was delighted and rushed off to
put it on.

Meanwhile Precious was inspecting the
table laid with chocolate cakes, muffins,
biscuits and steaming mugs of hot chocolate.
She sampled everything and shook her head
in wonder. "You *are* clever fairies – you
certainly don't need magic to help you!
Now, is Nina ready?"

Bella had put some large soft beanbags
in a semicircle on the floor by the window.
She asked everyone to sit there while Nina

took her place behind the silver curtains that Bella had draped over the forest mural.

Coriander pressed "Play" on the Daisy Discplayer, Bella drew back the curtains and Nina began her dance. The group of fairies watched her attentively as she interpreted the scene from *The Firebird*. As the music built up to its climax, Nina ran daintily across the room in a perfect pas couru and leaped confidently into the sissonne fondue,

ending in the graceful, melting fifth position just as she had planned.

The small audience jumped into the air, their wings whirring as they clapped and cheered, and Nina curtseyed.

"Well, well," said Precious, shaking her head in wonder. "You are a talent, Nina!" She asked Bella and Nyssa to come and stand next to Nina. "I have to say that this is a most original sleepover – I shouldn't think many fairies get to watch a stunning dance like that as their evening's entertainment! Bella, it was a wonderful idea of yours to invite your friends to earn their gems while staying with you. It shows true team spirit." The friends grinned at each other. "And you have been a marvellous hostess to these two as well," she added, looking at Poppy and Coriander. "Everyone has played a part in this lovely party. You deserved a second chance."

As she said this, she waved her wand, and the golden chains hanging round the

friends' necks glowed. Then the Glitter Club
President said the Gem Spell:

Emerald, sapphire, ruby, pearl –
One gem for each Glitter Girl!

The chains flashed with a bright light and a
gem appeared on the necklaces. Coriander
and Poppy gasped, for they too were now
wearing gold chains, each with a shining
pearl.

"Wow!" said Poppy, her eyes wide.
"How come we get a gem?"

"Those are special friendship gems,"
Precious explained. "They are not in
the Gem Book. I award them to fairies
who have helped their friends in times of
need. I think these two deserve them,
don't you?" she asked Bella and the
others.

"Too right!" cried Bella. "We wouldn't
have got our gems without their help."

"Actually, Bella, there's one more

thing you need our help with," said Poppy seriously.

"What's that?" asked Bella.

"Scoffing this lot!" cried Poppy, stuffing a whole muffin greedily into her mouth.

"Honestly, Poppy Dewdrop," said Nina wryly. "You are a handful!"

Log on to

Nina
Fairy Ballerina
.com

for magical games,
activities and fun!

Experience the magical world of
Nina and her friends at the Royal
Academy of Fairy Ballet. There are
games to play, fun activities to
make or do, plus you can learn more
about the Nina Fairy Ballerina books!

Log on to www.ninafairyballerina.com now!

Fairy Stories

Chosen by Anna Wilson

Every fairy has a story to tell

Be spirited away to fairyland and visit the wonderful worlds of dream fairies, funny fairy godmothers, a sweet-toothed cake fairy and a fairy who learns a lot about friendship.

This magical story collection is a must for all fairy fans.

Princess Stories

Chosen by Anna Wilson

Every princess has a story to tell.

A pretty perfect princess and a badly behaved princess, a princess in love and a princess in BIG trouble . . .

These are just a few of the princesses on parade in this fun, magical story collection.

A selected list of titles available from Macmillan Children's Books

The prices shown below are correct at the time of going to press. However, Macmillan Publishers reserves the right to show new retail prices on covers, which may differ from those previously advertised.

ANNA WILSON

NINA FAIRY BALLERINA

CHOSEN BY ANNA WILSON

All Pan Macmillan titles can be ordered from our website, www.panmacmillan.com, or from your local bookshop and are also available by post from:

Bookpost, PO Box 29, Douglas, Isle of Man IM99 1BQ
Credit cards accepted. For details:
Telephone: 01624 677237
Fax: 01624 670923
Email: bookshop@enterprise.net
www.bookpost.co.uk

Free postage and packing in the United Kingdom